Sharing

C000047031

Join the Travis Mayfair VIP Club:
Asian hotwife fun, delivered very discreetly to your
email.
No spam, no explicit emails, I don't share your address,
and you can unsubscribe anytime.
http://eepurl.com/gRZ04T

One

Yoona pressed her tight, slim body against me. She smelled like shampoo, expensive perfume, and the gin-and-tonic she'd just gulped down. In her skin-tight dress, writhing up against me, rubbing her thighs on my bulge in my crotch, every ounce of Yoona's being was sex. Even under Club Slam's blasting A/C, Yoona's gorgeous Korean face, her pert breasts, tight waist, bubble ass, and long legs radiated fiery heat.

That was the woman I married: way out of my league, looks-wise. Sexuality-wise. And she knew it.

Yoona? Pure Korean American sexuality, the kind of girl every guy stared at, whether in Los Angeles or Seoul.

Me? Just your average nerdy white guy graduate student. The kind of guy no girl stared at. The only time anybody stared at me was if I'd spilled coffee on my shirt.

Through her dress and my shirt, she rubbed her nipples all over my chest. My dick was hard. I was pouring sweat. She was grinding, dancing, pressing her bouncy push-up breasts into me. She rubbed her firm, toned thighs up against my dick.

I wasn't much of a dancer or clubber. It was one of those differences between us: those disparities we had found charming as boyfriend and girlfriend, and now were supposed to find even more charming as a newly married couple. I was introverted. She was extroverted. I was white. She was Korean. She liked to scream and party. I liked to read and think. She liked to fuck. I— I also liked to fuck, but I never could match Yoona's libido. No regular guy could.

She spent her weekend nights iatn the clubs, away from me, dancing and partying. Of course there were guys around. Good-looking guys. Popular guys. Rich guys. Manly guys. Guys who could kick my ass and laugh in my face as they pay off my student debt. I knew that.

I trusted Yoona. As famous as she was in Koreatown's club scene, she was always back in my bed right after the clubs closed. I was usually fast asleep by then.

Me? I spent my Friday nights reading. Studying. Going to Starbucks if I wanted to get wild.

She'd gone to college just to check off a box on her parents' wish list. Graduating from UCLA got her full access to the trust fund, the family penthouse condo in Gangnam, the beach house in Hawaii, and whatever else.

Me, I'd gone to college to do science. I was still doing science. We got married right after graduation, but I was still a student, although at least a *graduate* student.

I went clubbing once a year. Twice at most. It just wasn't my thing. It was very much Yoona's thing. She had the stunning looks, the hot body, and the bubbly personality for having fun clubbing. I didn't have any of those. But I didn't mind her enjoying herself. I didn't even mind her flirting a bit with other guys. As long as she followed the rules.

All the Chads and Brads, the cool rich guys, the athletes — they wanted my wife. Badly. And every night, after tempting them, teasing them, dancing with them, she'd come home to me. She'd slip into bed in the wee hours,

6

smelling like cologne and cigarettes and soju and cognac, and suck me off and fuck my brains out. Those other guys had spent the night nursing their hard-ons for her, but she was mine.

Of course she looked at them when she was out. I wasn't much to look at. She enjoyed checking them out. Looking at other men was fine. They looked back at her, stared at the woman who was my wife and my wife only, and I loved that.

Maybe she even danced with them. They got their hard-ons from her body and her smiles and her eyes and her smell. But that was as far as it went. Yoona never took it beyond that. I didn't have to tell her the specifics of how far she could go in the clubs. She knew.

On Yoona's birthday, BBD was performing at Slam. Big Boy Darnell. Superstar of gangsta rap. He had never heard of my wife Yoona Kim, but she'd definitely heard of him. He was her favorite. She had all his albums. I teased her that he was in town just for her birthday. In the club, him pumping and writhing in front of us, I had to remind myself that he wasn't actually in town for my wife's birthday, even if it really seemed like it. I even liked to ask her whether she thought BBD was sexy. That always made her turn red and flustered.

I'd saved up for three months so I could afford to take her out for her birthday. At least I could afford to pay for an Uber to the club. Uber Pool. And a few drinks while we were there. As long as they were few beers. Domestic beers. The cheapest ones.

7

She walked into the club as she owned it, strutting and pumping her ass through her skin-tight dress. She was my wife, but I hadn't realized how full and pert her breasts were. Her cleavage looked like a canyon of pleasure.

She was all mine. But other men would be staring. This time I'd be there to see it.

Yoona pushed her breasts up against me again. Shamelessly, she pulled her top open to give me — just me — a view. Her big, pert nipples were the color of ripe peaches. Her perfectly full, round breasts were the color of a big glass of milk with a dollop of honey in it.

Some startup-billionaire type guy with an upstyle that cost more than my rent blatantly stared at my wife. He danced closer and closer to her. She looked back over her shoulder at me, then started dancing with him.

He was obviously staring at every inch of her gorgeous body. I saw him. If he wasn't staring at her cleavage shaking to the beat, he was staring at how she pumped her ass as she danced.

As she was dancing, she rubbed her ass against his crotch. That couldn't have been accidental. His jaw dropped. She did it again. He was dripping sweat. She pushed her ass toward his crotch, then mounted his leg and slid her pussy up and down on it like it was a fire pole. His hands shook. He looked like he was about to cum from the feeling of my wife's body rubbing up against his.

He looked at her like he'd just been descended upon by the gods. She winked at him and stepped away, back into my arms. He was confused. He couldn't have the woman that would always be mine. I smiled at him, proudly.

Yoona turned her tight Asian ass toward my crotch. She rubbed against my dick slowly, sensuously, grinding it as she pumped her glutes in and out. I could imagine I was fucking her from behind. The upstyle-haired guy she'd been dancing with was no longer pretending not to stare at us; he was staring full-tilt. And I liked it.

Yoona's black hair flew in the air as she turned her head back at me. "He's here!" She screamed like a fangirl.

Yoona turned to face the club's stage. Her eyes were locked on the shirtless, tattooed hulk of a black man who'd just strutted onto the stage. That must've been the star: BBD. She was applauding his every step, as if everything he did was a miracle and worthy of applause.

BBD pointed at the DJ booth. The speakers beat like a drum. BBD started moving his body. He looked like a cobra, standing up, writhing, flexing his pulsating muscles, ready to strike. He was all six-foot-five of glistening, oiled-up muscle, with *BBD* tattooed across his hairy black chest. Big Boy Darnell.

Yoona looked back at me and screamed: "Oh my God, he's dancing!" She raised her arms in the air and applauded him.

Maybe a more normal woman would've been scared of his hypersexual presence. But my Yoona was enraptured. I wrapped my arms around her waist and tried to hold on to her just a little bit. She didn't even notice my arms around her. She focused her eyes on BBD.

BBD was supposedly the next Tupac. Or something like that. His first album had just sold triple-platinum. Even I, not following music news, knew that. He'd just received his twenty-million-dollar advance for his next album and had used it to buy his second house in Malibu. And Yoona was in love with him, at least as in love with him as she could be with a celebrity she'd never met in person.

All I could see was that he was huge: shirtless, muscular, tattooed, and oiled up. His muscles rippled as he moved. His presence and confidence were tremendous. Even if he hadn't been standing on stage shirtless, it would've been obvious that this man was a rich, muscular superstar: a man to be reckoned with. A man far manlier and more sexually desirable than I could ever hope to be.

Yoona pushed her hot little ass up against me. Her ass wasn't just beautiful-hot or sexy-hot. It was actually temperature-hot. I could feel its heat on my dick. Maybe she was all wound up sexually from the sight of a muscular, oiled-up rapper up on stage.

Her skin felt much warmer than it had been. Now my dick was even harder. She grabbed my hands and put them on top of her dress, right over her nipples.

The couple dancing next to us stared. Yoona's nipples hardened in my hands.

I had to fight my instincts and *not* pull my hands off her chest, *not* hide from the attention. I held her luscious soft breasts in my hands. I enjoyed the feeling of my dick growing super-hard as her tight Asian ass rubbed against it. I knew I was sweaty from the arousal.

Yoona pressed the curve of her back into my chest. She threw her head back, resting it on my shoulder, like she was cumming just from watching BBD strutting and writhing on stage. Yoona's beautiful black hair flew in my face. Her ass was all over my dick.

Her eyes were half-closed, like she was enjoying the moment, just being in BBD's aura. I knew she was aroused by him, not by me. That was life.

She turned her head back and grinned at me. "Feel how wet I am." Her grin looked just like she was the single hot girl on campus that somehow didn't chase me away. That grin. That grin when I'd first worked up the courage to ask her out to coffee. I couldn't believe my luck on that first Starbucks date with her.

She liked her coffee black. Black and strong. And hot.

"Feel it! I'm dripping!" I knew it: she was urging me to feel her pussy, showing off how horny the other man was making her.

"Wet? Is it raining in here? Where are you wet?" I wanted to hear her say it. I played dumb.

"My pussy." That was what I wanted to hear. It was direct.

She grabbed my hand and pulled it down to her thigh, then in under her dress. My palm slid over the impossibly smooth, soft Asian skin of her upper thigh, just as it turned into her soft, hairy pubic mound.

I held my finger erect as I slid it under her dress. It felt a few strands of her pubic hair, and her very wet labia lips. That pussy was soaking.

"Mmm." I nodded. "You're soaked."

"You can get your hand out of there now." She shook her head, giggled, and grabbed my wrist, like it didn't belong there. She completely pulled my hand out from under her dress and pushed it away, like she didn't want my hand anywhere near her pussy.

I sniffed my finger. It smelled like her juices. She rolled her eyes at me, like I was a pervert. Her eyes were on BBD the whole time. "God, I love watching him do his thing."

"BBD?" I asked. I was a little jealous. Maybe a lot jealous. *BBD, BBD...* it was all Yoona talked about. All she thought about. All she got wet for.

"Of course BBD!" She pushed her ass back onto my dick, then thrust it back and forth a few times, teasing my cocktip with her tight ass and the beginnings of her pussy. Her dress was tight enough for me to feel the difference. "Who else did you think I loved watching?"

"I don't know. Maybe, maybe—" I wasn't going to bring up myself, her husband. I wouldn't shame Yoona for complimenting BBD instead of me. I'd just let it go, as much as I could. I could live with that pang of jealousy. I even kind of liked it.

"BBD. I'm here for BBD, right?" She grinded her ass against my dick, teasing me just enough so I got super-hard, and no more than that. She knew my sexual capacity. She wouldn't let me get to orgasm. I knew I had no chance of cumming as she rubbed her hot little ass on me. She was all tease.

She glanced up at BBD, and at the front row full of rich guys who'd bought three-hundred-dollar bottles of champagne to sit close to the stage. She pouted at me. "Honey, will you buy us a bottle of champagne? I want a table closer to BBD. I want to have a better view."

I breathed deeply and looked around. At Slam, the most luxurious club in Koreatown, I was by far the poorest person in the room. I could afford this less than anyone else could. I probably made less than the janitor here. Yoona knew that. Maybe sometimes she forgot about it, or tried to make herself forget how weak I was in the money department.

Yoona was my wife. Of course she knew my finances were tight. I was just a graduate student. I wasn't like the rich guys she met in the club. She knew it already, but I dreaded having to talk about it again, and maybe sometimes she tried to make herself forget that she'd married a guy not just worse looking than her Koreatown peer group, but also much poorer.

"I'm sorry, Yoona. I only have enough for a few drinks. Actually just a few beers. Cheap beers. There's like sixty bucks in my wallet. My Visa's maxed out. I can't—" I shook my head. I felt bad, but reality was reality. I lived on a graduate student stipend, maxed-out credit cards, and a ton of student loans. The three twenties still in my wallet had to last all evening. Sixty dollars wouldn't even cover the expected hundred-dollar tip on bottle service at Slam.

"Oh, I'm sorry! I forgot." Yoona shook her head and laughed. Like my graduate-student poverty was funny. "I should've remembered." She winked and grinned like she knew something I didn't quite know, like she had some magic genie she could summon to get herself out of the conundrum — even if she wasn't going to take me along with her.

She turned away from me and turned to BBD dancing on stage. The dude's muscles rippled like ocean waves. He preened like a snake about to strike its prey. He wore thick gold chains that were themselves like snakes wrapped around his neck. Those chains were worth more than my annual stipend. He could've bought Yoona a bottle of champagne and not even noticed it. Was Yoona also thinking that?

The club's spotlights on BBD's oiled-up black skin made his body look luminous. Almost supernatural. A muscular god strutting before his supplicants. He was at least six foot five, conservatively speaking. He had muscles everywhere. Maybe a solid two eighty, all muscle. Even his neck looked like a huge muscle.

I didn't dare to think about what his dick must've looked like. But I couldn't help but notice its outline in his basketball shorts. There was no way not to see it. He wasn't hiding his size. The bulge extended down his thigh. It ran almost down to his knee.

BBD held his arms over his head. Damn. His biceps and triceps could crush mortals. His pecs were like cannons on a fighter jet: very credible warnings.

BBD was tattooed right on his chest. As if anyone doubted who he was. Or what he was packing.

The rings in his nipples were like asterisks on the *BBD* tattooed on his chest. I'd never seen a stud like this. Even his bushy black armpit hair was incredibly manly. It was the first time I'd ever felt inadequate about my armpit hair. But even in that piddling category, this man was by far my superior.

Sure, I knew some macho guys at the UCLA chemistry labs. Even some black guys. But none of them were anywhere like this dude.

His arms over his head, he writhed, more and more like a python about to pounce. Yoona was enthralled. She'd gone from pressing her ass firmly into my crotch to dancing a good foot away from me.

My wife raised her arms over her head, dancing just like BBD. She knew how that made her breasts stand out. She was already wearing a low-cut dress. When she danced like that, her boobs looked incredibly delicious. She stared at him as she danced. She was shaking and strutting at him, like she was presenting her tits to him.

BBD wore sunglasses on stage, but he was obviously staring at my wife. I could almost see his lusty eyes through his shades. He pointed at Yoona as he danced. It was his mating call.

I turned red. From behind, I put my hands on my wife's sides as she danced. She shook me off like she was shaking off dirty. She was totally focused on the man on stage.

He ran his hand over his dick on top of his shorts. He was blatant. His fingertips ran over every curve of his dick. I could even tell where he was circumcised.

I wasn't the kind of guy to check out other dudes' equipment. But this guy — there was no way not to notice his equipment. He had not only size but also confidence. And he was showing it off to my wife.

Yoona smiled at him as she slid her long, slim finger into her mouth. She sucked on it. Then she pulled her finger out of her mouth, her saliva dripping from the bright red polish of her fingernail, and she reached out and pretended to touch BBD with that finger.

"Sssss! Sizzling hot!" she screamed at him, and giggled, like it was just a joke. I felt small.

He started dancing like he was thrusting his dick at her. It wasn't dancing as much as it was air-fucking. I even saw the outline of his huge balls swinging inside his shorts as he did his mating dance for my wife.

I didn't dare lay my hands on Yoona. She was dancing, pulsating, pumping, and gyrating just for him. I stared at her tight, shapely Asian ass, the same ass that had first attracted me when I'd seen her on the UCLA campus years back. Now her tight, muscular Korean ass was pumping in the air like she was fucking BBD right there in the club.

She parted her legs just a little. She licked her finger. Then slipped it right under her dress. She moaned and laughed. Her finger must've been in her pussy. She took her finger out of her pussy, slowly licked it while looking at BBD, and pretended to extend it out to him again. "Shhh! Super-hot!" She made that same sizzling sound, but now she shut her eyes as she did it. Her head shuddered like she was in the middle of orgasm.

"Hey in the back row. What's up." BBD smiled a huge smile at my wife. From his vantage point above us up on stage, he pointed directly at her. His hairy black hand pointing at Yoona was like a call from the heavens. His teeth sparkled white. His smile looked genuinely friendly and inviting, at least toward her. To me it looked threatening.

"Oh my God! He noticed me!" Yoona giggled. "BBD, I love you!"

I gulped air and tried to calm myself down. She was just having some fun on her birthday. It was part of who she was, and who I wasn't. I always let her have a bit of fun. I knew she was out at the clubs often. But it had never gone this far.

"What's up, my gorgeous Asian lady?" BBD faced her as he danced. He flexed and rolled his abs while he stared at her and danced and writhed. He was definitely showing off. He held up his arms again and flexed the right, then the left. He was totally shameless. Those muscles. And that damn bushy black armpit hair again. He was pure testosterone.

He took off his sunglasses. I was right: he was staring directly at her.

I panicked. I couldn't buy a bottle. Even if I used up all the cash I had, even if I somehow pawned my watch, I couldn't buy a bottle. I could at least buy another drink for Yoona.

"Can I buy you a drink?" I shouted to her. It was like yelling at a stranger. She was standing only a few feet away, but all her attention was on BBD's muscles. And probably his dick.

"What?" She looked back at me with a smile and a head-shake, like I'd just proposed the most ridiculous thing.

"I mean, I'd like to buy you a drink. What would you like? Rum and Coke? Raspberry martini? Anything you like." I reached out to her and patted her sides. Drinks cost right near twenty bucks. I'd still have enough left over for us to get home.

"Oh, it's alright, Danny. I know you can't afford it." Yoona waved her hand. She waved away my offer, my worth as a husband, my masculinity.

"I can afford a drink," I shouted at Yoona through the club's pumping noise. BBD strutted up on stage, pumping his

"Uh, I believe it's—" the bartender frantically paged through the bar's bottle menu. "I need to check what it's called, but it's gonna be expensive—"

"I can afford it. Money ain't no problem when I'm buying for a lady like this." BBD pointed at my wife and laughed and shook his head. "Damn. She's hot. Get a table up here on stage. And a bottle of your most expensive bub."

"Yes, sir." The bartender nodded eagerly.

"Bub?" I mouthed silently and shook my head.

"Champagne. He ordered champagne." Yoona clicked her tongue, rolled her eyes, and shook her head, all at once. "You don't know?"

Was I really so clueless and out of touch?

BBD nodded at the bartender, then looked at my wife again. "And I want that gorgeous Asian lady with the face and body to match, the sexy birthday girl with the long legs and the lustrous black hair, up here on stage with me."

"Me?" Yoona looked genuinely surprised. She looked back at me. For the first time, it looked like she wasn't sure what to do. "Really, you want me up on stage with you?"

"Unless you're gonna turn down BBD." He made a sad face like an emoji, then laughed again, raucously. He never thought she'd turn him down. No woman ever turned him down.

He laughed into the microphone. It was that same laugh like a rapper who'd just made hundred-dollar bills rain. Except this rapper was only making my wife's pussy rain.

"I can't turn down BBD!" Yoona squealed, laughing.

She glanced again back at me over her shoulder, then started to say something to BBD. "But my husband—" Then she shrugged and waved her hand at me, like I was a bothersome instinct.

She was waving away my very existence. She didn't even wait for my answer. I was utterly powerless.

Yoona didn't walk up on stage. She ran.

I only stared at the outline of her perfect ass walking away from me, her gorgeous black hair down her lithe back, and her toned legs getting farther and farther away. She looked like pure sex as she climbed the stairs to the stage. BBD was waiting for her.

The bartender set a bottle of champagne and two glasses in front of BBD and my wife.

"Whoa." BBD stared her up and down, from her gorgeous Asian hair to her almond eyes to her red lips to her milky white cleavage to her tight, toned body and her long legs. "You're even hotter up close. You got *sex* written all over you. In neon marker."

Yoona laughed again. "You're hot too!" She said to him. "Even hotter up close."

She licked her finger and held it out. This time she was so close to him. Would she actually touch him? She pressed the finger into his chest, right where his tattoo said *BBD*. She shrieked before she could even make a sizzling noise.

"Oh my God! I touched BBD's chest!" She made a loud sizzling sound, pretended to be shaking and electrified in rhythm to the beat of BBD's music, and smiled at the audience. It was like she was showing off her infidelity.

She fanned herself. It didn't look like an act. I saw the beads of sweat on her forehead. She was electrified by just having laid her finger on this black stud's thick, pulsating body. Her cheeks flushed red and her forehead dripped sweat.

I knew that look on Yoona's face: she was horny as fuck. Through her tight dress, above her gorgeous Asian legs, her pink, swollen pussy lips dripped for BBD.

Two

"Just remember." BBD put his arms around my wife as he spoke into the microphone. His hands cupped the tight little hemispheres of her firm Asian ass. "Every song I'm performing here, it's all for you, birthday girl."

Yoona took a sip of champagne. She was cooing at the guy. "I feel so special now. I've never had a birthday like this." She stared at him like he was Mickey Mouse and she'd just arrived in Disneyland.

She sipped her champagne again, then sniffed it deeply. "My hubby can't afford expensive things like this. He can barely buy me a beer." She laughed, then shook her head. She didn't even look down at me. She was inhaling the champagne's scent, or BBD's. I could only imagine how strongly he smelled of sweat, body oil, and strong black precum.

Yoona smiled. Whatever she was smelling satisfied her. She spoke into his big black microphone. "Most delicious thing I've ever tasted." She took a big gulp of the champagne, looking at BBD the whole time.

"Yeah, you like that?" He laughed. She nodded eagerly, then tipped the champagne glass over her mouth, so the last few drops fell onto her tongue. She swallowed them one by one, licked her lips, and smiled at BBD, like the champagne wasn't quite enough.

The bartender ran up on stage and refilled her champagne glass, then held up his hand and excused himself.

BBD moved his hands from her ass cheeks to her hips. He kept dancing like he was thrusting his dick into her.

"What's your name, gorgeous lady?" He held the big black microphone up to her red lips.

"Yoona." She stared into his eyes. She looked like she wanted to kiss the tip of that microphone. "Yoona Kim."

"Aw, baby." BBD laughed. He ran a hand down my wife's face and smiled. "You're Korean?"

"Yes! Oh my God, how did you know?" Yoona giggled.

BBD said something incomprehensible to her. He was totally confident when he said it, like it was a secret code he was sure she'd understand.

My wife covered her mouth and giggled. She did actually understand.

He said something incomprehensible again.

Did they actually have some secret language between them?

My wife covered her mouth again and shook her head in disbelief. She spoke into his microphone: "Oh my God, how do you know Korean?"

BBD shrugged. His gargantuan shoulder and arm muscles rippled even when he shrugged. "I was in the Army. Stationed in Korea for a few years. Thought I'd might as well pick up the language when I was over there."

Yoona squealed. "It's so hard!" She covered her mouth. "I mean Korean! The language is so difficult! My husband can't speak a word of it."

"Yeah, well." BBD ran his hand through my wife's sheen black hair. "I'm not your husband." He laughed.

She reached out, red fingernails and all, and squeezed at his bicep. Her slim Asian hand could barely cover the bulge of muscle on his arm. She nodded in approval at his body of thick, bulky muscle. "I'm sure you were a sex god over there. You'd be a sex god anywhere. Especially here." She blushed more. "I'm sure the girls over there loved you."

BBD shook his head. "I never saw any girls over there as hot as you, Yoona."

"Oh my God!" My wife fanned herself with her hand and gulped more champagne. The number of times she said *oh my God*, it was like she was having an orgasm up on stage. "I can't believe you'd think I'm hot."

"Oh, you're obviously hot, Yoona. Yoona, right? That's your name?"

"Yes, Yoona!" She smiled at him, then reached out with her other hand to squeeze his other big black bicep. It was just as thick. She was just as impressed. "And what can I call you?" She spoke into the microphone. "Do I call you BBD?"

"You can call me BBD if you want." He laughed and looked down at the bulge in his crotch. He patted it like it was his pet cobra. "But my name is Darnell."

She grabbed both of his biceps and pressed up against him, dancing and pushing her tight Asian body up against him. She'd danced with me when we'd just arrived at the club, but it wasn't anything like that.

"Ooh, Darnell!" She squeezed his bicep again, as if she was making sure he wasn't just a sexual fantasy she was having. "I love your name!"

What the fuck did that even mean? She loved the name *Darnell*? Had she forgotten all about *Danny*? Her husband?

BBD folded his hands behind his head as he danced, showing off his muscles, his huge shirtless chest, and his manly armpit hair. "Yeah, baby. I'm here to please you." The audience cheered him on.

Yoona stared him up and down as he strutted through his next song. She started by paying equal attention to his whole muscular body, from his high-tops, his pumped-up calves, his big ass, his muscled torso, his huge arms and shoulders — but by the end of the song she was staring only at his dick.

BBD stood next to her. He wrapped his arm around her from behind, then slipped his finger down her back. She shivered and giggled. He finished by squeezing one of her ass cheeks, and lightly slapping the other one.

Yoona didn't say anything. She bit her lower lip and stared down at BBD's dick.

"Alright, the next song." BBD laughed. "The next song is kind of a classic. If you can excuse a bit of vulgarity, you know what I'm saying, Yoona? Yoona, can you excuse me using a bit of rough language?"

Yoona was dancing and staring down at his dick. It was like she didn't hear his words. The sight of his dick, even just through his shorts, hypnotized her.

"Yoona! Wake up!" I yelled toward the stage.

She snapped and looked up at me.

"Is that your husband?" BBD looked at me, then at her.

Yoona nodded. She shrugged, as if she was apologizing for my existence.

BBD said something in Korean to her. Yoona looked at me and laughed. She actually doubled over laughing, covering her mouth and looking at me. When she finished laughing, she wagged her finger at BBD. "You naughty boy, you."

"You bring out the naughty in me, baby." He rubbed up against her. He was obviously making sure to rub his dick against her body. She must've felt his dick bulge even through her tight dress. "So as I was saying, can you excuse a bit of my naughty language in my next song?"

"I can excuse anything," Yoona said. As she spoke, her eyes didn't leave BBD's crotch.

"Alright, alright." BBD clapped his hands above his head. He scratched his chest and I noticed how hairy that chest was: that blackness wasn't just his skin, but the black hair all over him. He scratched his chest like a huge, hung gorilla. "This next song is called — Yoona, you wanna hear what this song is called?"

"I want it," Yoona said to him. "Give it all to me, Darnell."

She kneeled in front of him. She was staring straight ahead at his dick, like she was going to worship it.

"Next song is called." BBD cleared his throat. "Next song is one of my classics. Taking it back to the old school, back to 2017. It's called *Suck My Big Black Dick*." He laughed. "Is that your husband there in the back row?"

"Yeah." Yoona nodded, and shrugged. Like I was an afterthought.

"Alright, alright." BBD reached out and ran his big black hand through Yoona's silky smooth hair. "This song's dedicated to your husband."

"Oh my God!" Yoona looked up at his face, then straight ahead at the bulge in his crotch. Even from my position far from the stage, my wife's smile was unmistakable.

BBD pumped his fist in the air. "Suck My Big Black Dick!"

Three

"Hear what I said? Suck my big black dick." BBD raised his arm and pumped his fist to the crowd. They cheered and applauded. My wife was kneeling in front of him, staring into his crotch — as if it held the secrets of the universe.

The rhythm section started, electronic drum beats and samples like jungle music. BBD preened like he was strutting around the stage, but actually he stood still. He strutted with his face and his arms, gesturing to the room. He even strutted with his cocky grin and rippling muscles from his calves all the way up to his neck. He gyrated his crotch toward my wife's face.

The basketball shorts on his dick looked like a thin shroud on a skyscraper. The contents were way too obvious. I'd never stared at a dude's dick. But this dude's dick, I couldn't ignore. It demanded attention. And a little bit of fear.

Smiling up at him, my wife reached up to the waistband of his shorts. He looked down and smiled back at her. She pulled down slowly. He was dancing, pumping, gyrating.

My wife pulled the front of his shorts down enough for his bushy black hair to make itself known.

She kept taking his shorts down. Down and down. Until the base of his dick emerged: all black thickness. Even from my position in the back of the room, I could see its size, and the big veins popping out of it at the base.

"Oh my God!" There was her catchphrase again. She screamed it up at BBD. She'd so far revealed only the base of his dick. Maybe the first few inches. "Oh my God, it looks like a cobra."

"Yeah. My cobra." BBD smiled and nodded, like he heard that every day. He pumped his fist in the air again, flexing his biceps and triceps. "Suck my big black dick." The crowd cheered.

"It's—" Yoona slid his shorts down farther. She gasped. "Jesus Christ!"

"Nah, just BBD." He laughed like her shock wasn't exactly surprising.

"I don't even—" Yoona slid his shorts far down enough to see the blood-purple cockhead atop his huge black dick.

The whole schlong sprung out and pointed at her face: the purple head, glistening with precum, the neatly trimmed foreskin, and the huge, veiny black shaft that disappeared into BBD's forest of black pubes.

That thick black shaft must've been ten inches long, and thick like a Starbucks cup. Except it definitely wasn't white. And Yoona wasn't drinking from it, yet.

BBD's bushy black pubic hair surrounded the base of his dick. Below his pubes, his balls hung low and swung loosely. Above his manly pubes, his muscular thighs and abs announced their intention to pump that dick deep into my wife, just as his balls announced his sex drive and fertility.

Framed by those masculine pubes and muscular thighs and abs, his black cock looked even bigger than it was. If I had to guess just from the sight of it, I would've guessed it was twenty inches long. I knew that would've been physically impossible. But his big black dick sure looked like a twenty-incher. I felt small all over.

My wife reached out to his dick. She wrapped her delicate Asian fingers around it and held it up to her face. She sniffed it.

She smiled up at him. She must have loved the musky smell of his pubes and sweet invitation of his precum. She put her gorgeous face up to his dick and just rubbed her face against it: her cheeks, her nose, her chin, even her forehead. It was like those Europeans who rubbed noses when they kissed, except Yoona rubbed her whole face all over this dude's big black dick.

She held the cockhead up to her lips. Blazing spotlights lit up the crown of glistening precum on the tip of BBD's dick.

"Can I?" Yoona asked him.

"You don't have to ask me permission." BBD laughed. "Anyway, what's the song called? I believe it's called *Suck My Big Black*— "

He didn't even finish his words. Yoona went down on him. A good six inches of his shaft were already in her tight little Asian mouth. She looked up at him for approval.

"Yeah, that's the idea." He nodded and laughed. He laid his hands on his hips and looked down to watch my wife furiously working his dick. She slurped at his dickhead, then with her tongue traced every vein on his dick, from the base to the tip.

BBD moaned and nodded as she worked her tight red Korean lips up and down his dick. The crowd was entranced.

They were cheering. I found myself cheering too — even though this was my wife sucking another man's dick, a big black stranger's dick. I found it just as thrilling as everyone else found it. Or maybe a lot more thrilling. Yoona wasn't their wife, after all. She was my wife. Or she had been my wife. Now she was worshipping a rap star's huge black dick.

BBD stared down at my wife. "Baby, you're beautiful."

She slipped his dickhead out of her mouth and stared at his shaft. He brought his big black microphone down near her mouth. She looked up at him and said softly into the microphone: "Darnell, you're beautiful too. I mean, you're the most handsome man I've ever. I mean—" And she pushed his dick back into her mouth.

She was moaning loudly enough for the crowd to hear. She was taking most of his shaft into her mouth, all but the last two or three inches.

BBD said something in Korean into the microphone, then laughed.

Yoona looked up at him and nodded. She opened her right Asian mouth wide, extra wide, and leaned her head back like she was sitting in the chair at the dentist's office. A big, black dentist's office.

BBD loaded his dick into her mouth. First just half the shaft. Then, inch by inch, more of it. And then more.

"You doing ok there, Yoona?" he asked while looking down at her.

My wife nodded frantically, as if being deprived of the rest of his black dick was what she most feared in life.

She laid one of her delicate hands on BBD's hairy ass cheek. She was squeezing it and pulling him closer, urging him to load more of his black dick into her. As she moaned, she ran the fingertips of her left hand over his hairy black balls — it looked like she was playing piano, the way she quickly, lightly moved her fingers on BBD's huge, hairy nuts. Her red fingernails disappeared into the deep jungle of his manly black pubes.

He rested one hand on his hip. With the other hand, he played with my wife's lustrous Asian hair, exactly the same way I'd played with her hair on our first Starbucks date back in college. She was only looking up at him and smiling in satisfaction as she sucked hard on his dick.

She took her hand off his ass cheek and smacked it once. Loud. BBD asked her something in Korean. The Korean guys in the crowd looked shocked. What had he just said? Yoona nodded eagerly. She spread her knees farther apart and wrapped her slim, bare arms around the thick black trunks of BBD's legs.

"If y'all wondering what I just said." BBD laughed and nodded as he spoke into the microphone. "I just told this Korean girl that I wanna fuck her face." He laughed. Like it was just a normal thing to say to my wife. He continued talking. "And she seems pretty happy about the idea."

He pulled a strand of hair out of Yoona's face and looked down to her. He asked something else in Korean. The Korean guys in the club laughed. Yoona nodded eagerly.

"If y'all wondering again," BBD announced into the microphone. His voice boomed authoritatively through the club, like Zeus speaking down from the heavens. "If y'all wondering. I just said I'm gonna cum in her tight little Korean mouth. She seems pretty happy about it."

BBD squinted and looked back at me in the back of the club. "Yoona's hubby, how do you feel about that? That I'm gonna fuck your wife's face and shoot my black seed into her pretty little Asian mouth?"

I shrugged.

"You alright with that?" BBD smiled confidently and pointed a big black finger right at me. It might as well have been his dick.

I didn't know what to say. I didn't even know how I felt, other than that I simultaneously felt humiliated and on top of the world.

"Yeah, that's what I expected." BBD nodded at me and laughed. "Hubby doesn't have much of an opinion on the matter of me face-fucking his wife."

I caught a glimpse of Yoona's eyes. She didn't see me.

Her entire being was focused on the man, the crotch, and the dick immediately in front of her. I'd never seen her so full of desire. Her face as she stared at BBD's dick and grabbed at his ass cheeks was pure lust. She wanted him to face-fuck her. Badly. She'd never wanted anything from me so badly. She'd never even looked at me like that, not even on our honeymoon.

BBD backed his shaft out of my wife's mouth slowly, deliberately, like he was cocking a spring-loaded weapon. Then he smiled, gleaming white teeth everywhere, with traces of gold grills reflecting off the club's spotlights. His gold grills must've been worth more than my Kia.

He shoved his dick into my wife's mouth so hard that I feared it would knock her down. Yoona wasn't fazed. She loved it. She nodded eagerly as she slobbered over his dick and pawed at his ass and balls. Her cute little Asian nose was stuck in the midst of his forest of manly black pubes.

She gulped. The bulge in her throat — was that the tip of BBD's dick? It must've been. The bulge in her throat went away when BBD pulled his dick away, then the came back when he again shoved his dick into my wife's eager mouth. He shoved his big black microphone near her face so the club could hear her moans of raw pleasure as this rich, strong, muscular black man face-fucked my wife.

Yoona never acted this sexual with me. I just didn't elicit that in her.

I could only imagine: getting face-fucked by BBD was finally fulfilling her fantasy for a man more masculine than I was, with a bigger dick than mine, a better salary than mine, a nicer body than mine. This dude even spoke fluent Korean. He was my superior to me in every possible way. Yoona deserved him.

I no longer suspected Yoona was embarrassed to be sucking another man's dick on stage. She must've been embarrassed only by my company.

BBD didn't groan as he fucked my wife. He roared.

Even without his microphone, he growled into the club. The audience was enthralled. They'd come for an exhibition of his masculinity, even if this was a bit more than they'd expected.

His veiny dick pounded my wife's mouth like a jackhammer. When I dared to squint and stare to get a look at the details, I could make out drops of his glistening precum dripping down Yoona's chin.

She'd brought her hand under her dress; she must've been frantically fingering herself while this big black stud shoved his dick in my wife's mouth.

"Aw yeah!" BBD pumped his fist in the air. His biceps and triceps looked like he could beat the shit out of anybody, even the club bouncers. "I'm a gonna cum now."

BBD closed his eyes and bit his blood-red lower lip. His dickhead was the same color as his lip. He grabbed my wife's hair as he face fucked her. She nodded in pleasure. He roared again and slowed down his fucking. He threw his head back. His big red nipples stood up. Sweat poured down his face.

His ass cheeks pumped and his thighs tightened. "Awww yeah!" He shouted at the crowd and pumped his fist again. Everyone was in awe; this hypersexual stud was very near climax, and my precious Asian wife was right there to take his hot black seed.

Yoona's face turned to shock for a full half-second. Her cheeks filled up. She looked like a chipmunk. She smiled up at him. She spread her crotch farther; she was furiously finger-fucking herself while swallowing this strange man's seed deep inside her.

Gulp. Gulp again. She swallowed his cum. The gobs of his hot black seed made big bulges in her tiny little Asian throat as she eagerly drank it down.

BBD's lower body quivered again. He was shooting more of his fertile black nectar into her. Yoona's cheeks filled up again. My wife swallowed his cum again and smiled up at him happily.

She opened her mouth. Some thick white cream dripped out of her red lips onto her cleavage. She giggled and looked up at BBD. "Thank you, Darnell."

"Aw, yeah." BBD nodded down at her, like he'd just done her a big favor. Maybe he had. I didn't have that kind of dick. I didn't have that kind of fucking power. I couldn't even buy my wife a bottle of champagne.

called 'Fuck It.' You know what I'm saying here, Mister White Husband?"

BBD laughed uproariously.

My wife held one slim, nail-polished finger up to BBD's mouth. He licked it, slowly. She rubbed her crotch up against him, then slipped that same finger up under her dress. She half closed her eyes, half left them open and stared at the oiled-up, hyper-masculine black man standing there in front of her as she fingered herself.

"Should this song go out to Mister Hubby again?" BBD stared at me like he was looking for an answer. I shrugged. I didn't know. It was his song. It was his show. It was his everything.

BBD snapped his fingers in the air. "So this song, it goes a little like this—" He nodded his head and the beat machines started.

"Urgggghhhh!" BBD growled into the microphone. He rolled his ab muscles and pumped the air with his crotch, like he was fucking the air conditioner. "Fuck it!"

My wife sat down on the stage floor. Its surface was shiny black. If I stared hard enough, I could see up her skirt in the mirror-black reflection.

She drew out her slim, toned Asian legs, to give BBD a full view. She raised her finger from her pussy to her mouth again, took a long lick, then brought her finger back down to her pussy and kept fingering herself.

BBD grabbed at her dress. He pulled it off of her in one quick motion. I had never seen anyone do that. I never would've been able to undress my own wife that quickly, and I'd seen her wear that dress a million times before.

She lay there in her bra and panties, still fingering herself. She had two fingers inside. With her left hand she was grabbing at her own breasts.

"Bartender!" BBD yelled again. He snapped his fingers in the air. "I need a condom over here."

"Yes, sir!" The bartender reached into a shelf over his head.

"No! No condom!" My wife shook her head vigorously. She made an X with her arms. "I want Darnell's seed in my pussy."

BBD shook his head. "Honey, I don't wanna be paying no child support for eighteen years here. I know your husband can't afford to raise my baby."

"I'm on birth control!" Yoona grabbed her purse at the side of the stage and waved a plastic pill box at him.

"Alright, alright." He laughed and nodded. "Just make sure your birth control works against strong black cum. I ain't shootin' no apple juice here."

"Oh, yes!" Yoona's words came like moans. She was still fingering herself, half-naked on the gleaming black club floor. She shook the birth control pill box at BBD one more time. "No condom, ok? Bareback me. Cum in me, Big Boy Darnell."

That was Yoona. She didn't take risks. She wouldn't risk missing out on getting pumped full of Big Boy Darnell's fertile seed.

She sat up. She reached out and grabbed at BBD's shorts. She succeeded to pull them down just a little. He just looked more like a gangsta rapper.

41

I stared at the curve of her back, her lustrous black hair, and her firm breasts in hre bra. Her body was a volcano of lust. Watching her from feet away was like being at a strip club, except Yoona was much hotter than any woman I'd seen at a strip club. And she was about to get fucked on stage.

BBD was on the floor, on all fours. My wife moaned, her legs up in the air.

She'd forgotten to take off her panties. Or she knew how quick BBD was at it. One swoop with his big black hand and her panties were off. Another swoop and her bra was also gone.

BBD rose to kneeling and smiled at me. His brilliant white teeth were like blinding spotlights. "You may want to have a sniff if you miss your wife." He balled up the bra and panties and smiled as he looked down at them, then looked at me.

Still kneeling, he pumped his big muscular arm. He threw like a fastball pitch. Hard. Too hard and fast for me to see it coming.

My wife's panties and underwear hit me in the forehead, then bounced down onto the table in front of me, limply covering my glass of apple juice.

"Thanks." I nodded to him. It was all I could do.

He laughed at me and gave me a thumbs-up. Yoona grabbed at his shorts again. She pulled down. I saw more of the base of his shaft. My wife kept pulling down on his shorts.

She squealed like a fangirl when his tremendous black schlong popped out. She actually applauded his dick popping out of his shorts and pointing at her crotch as the black stud kneeled next to her.

Who applauds a stranger's penis? My wife, apparently.

From just a few feet away, I could actually smell his black cock's manly essence: all pheromones, precum, and the remnants of salty cum he'd already shot into my wife's mouth.

Still kneeling, BBD completely took off his shorts. Even a naturally awkward maneuver like that, he wasn't awkward in doing. I would've fallen all over myself if I ever tried to take off my shorts while kneeling. I could barely change my shoes while standing up.

My wife grabbed his shorts off of him. Her motions were so natural, like she was completely at ease undressing a hot black stud as her husband watched.

She looked down into his shorts and stuck her face in them. She inhaled deeply and smiled directly at me.

Still half sitting up, my wife pulled her arm back and threw BBD's basketball shorts right at my face. Yoona had played baseball — not softball — in college, and it showed. BBD's shorts hit me in the face, again. I tried to take the hit gracefully. I was more interested in seeing the action on stage than lamenting my inability to catch the underwear of my wife and her new lover.

"In case you're wondering how a real man's dick smells!" Yoona laughed and went back to staring at BBD's dick. She kept playing with herself, frantically flicking her hot little Asian clit while she looked at the monstrous, perfectly hard black schlong BBD was going to shove into her.

Yoona knew exactly how BBD's dick smelled. She'd already lovingly pressed her face up to it. She also knew how it tasted. She'd sucked it, slobbered all over it, savored every part of that black dick on her tongue. She only hadn't taken his dick in her tight Asian pussy. That part was about to change.

A tuft of her black pubic hair lay over her clit. I always got hard seeing that beautiful straight black Asian pubic hair. Back in college, that was my sign I was going to get some action with gorgeous Yoona Kim. Now it was the sign that a strange man was going to get some action with gorgeous Yoona Kim.

As she flicked her clit back and forth, her body flushed red. Her breasts matched the red of her pussy lips and her polished fingernails. Her pale honey-yellow skin was turning red in all her erogenous zones.

Her nipples stood up and shone bright flaming pink. I'd never seen them that erect or that pink. She'd never been that aroused by me.

BBD was kneeling next to her. His big black ass muscles looked like they were made for thrusting into other men's wives. His bush of pubes looked like a big black jungle. His balls looked like they could on their own regenerate the entire black race. He held unspeakable quantities of hot, fertile black cum. His dick dripped precum as he held it in the direction of her tight pussy.

"No condom, right?" Yoona asked him, just to double-check. "Please, no condom!"

"No condom." BBD laughed. "I've never barebacked a hot little Asian bitch."

"Oh yeah." Yoona moaned in pleasure and lay down flat on her back. "I love it when you talk dirty like that."

If I'd ever called Yoona a *hot little Asian bitch*, she would've slapped me, then divorced me. BBD was allowed certain liberties I wasn't allowed. I'd never be allowed. He was my superior in every way.

Yoona spread her legs, knees up, like she was in a gynecologist's office. With her lithe fingers, she pulled her pussy lips apart. She smiled at BBD. It was an invitation. He was no gynecologist, but he'd definitely make my wife's pussy feel good.

"Gotta warn you." BBD laughed and looked in my direction. "If that's your husband, you're probably not used to a real man's dick."

"I can learn!" BBD's dick wasn't even near her pussy yet but Yoona winced and bit down on her arm to prepare for it. She blinked her gorgeous almond-shaped eyes and moaned.

"Alright, I'ma be gentle with you." Still kneeling, BBD walked closer to her, on his knees. Even doing that, he didn't look one bit awkward. He had to hold up his erect dick so it wasn't sullied by touching the floor.

"Deep. Go as deep as you can." Suddenly Yoona threw her legs up in the air. It was almost comical, circus-like. Her body really looked like the letter Y with her hot, toned legs up in the air just waiting for the black man's dick in her pussy.

"Aw, shit." BBD laughed and shook his head. "You must be starving for a dick bigger than three inches."

"My husband is—" Yoona looked embarrassed. She shook her head. Her gorgeous hair swung back and forth. "I don't wanna talk about my husband. Just fuck me deep, Darnell."

"Shit." BBD put one hairy black finger next to my wife's tight Asian hole. "You really think I can fit my dick in here?"

"I want you to shove it in my hole." Yoona was almost shouting.

She never talked to me like that. She grabbed BBD's dick like it was a fire hose and the whole city was in flames. She rubbed his engorged purple-red-black cockhead up and down on her pussy lips.

"You almost ready—?" BBD started to ask her.

Yoona thrust her whole lower body toward BBD's dick. It went inside her. She gasped, then moaned in pleasure.

"Oh fuck." BBD shook his head and smiled down at me. "Your wife is so fucking hungry for my dick."

"I guess I haven't—" I started to explain. "Maybe I haven't been satisfying— Sometimes I—"

BBD wasn't listening to me. His dick was inside my wife. He pushed it in even more. Yoona pulled him in closer, her red fingernails on his big black ass cheeks. Sweat poured down off his face and chest onto my gorgeous Asian wife's firm, taut body.

"Fuck me!" Yoona yelled. The crowd cheered.

BBD mounted her like a bull fucking a cow in heat. He sped up his rhythm: in and out of her tight Asian pussy as she moaned and grabbed at his big black ass cheeks to try to get him deeper in her.

BBD's eyes were closed. His whole muscular body rippled as he pumped his long, thick dick into her. His hands roamed over her body as if he owned it: he pawed at her tits, pulled on her nipples, ran his hand over her tight abs, and even slapped her ass cheeks. She moaned in pleasure louder the more BBD's big black hands fondled her tight body. When he slapped her ass, she let out a special high-pitched moan. The only time I'd heard her moaning like that was when she was using her vibrator. I could never satisfy her like that.

His shaft jackhammered her so fast that all I saw was a blur. His sweat was everywhere, dripping from BBD's black hairy chest and armpits all over my wife's pristine soft Asian skin. His low-hanging black balls collided with her tight little ass every time he thrust into her. Not that I was an expert on balls, but I'd never seen balls remotely that huge on any dude at the gym. But then, dudes at the gym didn't fuck my wife. As far as I knew.

BBD's black shaft pounding my wife's pussy sounded like a wet jackhammer. She wrapped her legs around his torso, pulled on his ass cheeks, and fondled his black balls. She was loving it. All I could hear from her moans was "Don't stop!"

I sipped my apple juice. I was left out, cheated, abandoned, forsaken.

But my dick was hard. I was ashamed of my wife being fucked by a stranger. But what I was even more ashamed of was that I liked it.

She was reaching sexual heights I'd never seen. BBD was doing exactly what I was incapable of doing for her. I was seeing exactly the man I could never be.

Every few seconds, Yoona opened her eyes and stared at the big muscular torso of the stud who was powerfucking her. She smiled at him every time. With her dainty feet resting on his back and her lithe red fingernails on his hairy black ass cheeks, pulled him in a little closer to her.

He slid his hands under her ass, to bring her up closer as he was fucking her. She was pushing her pussy in toward him every time he thrust his dick into her. She looked like she was putting more effort into taking him deeper into her than he was. BBD looked like he'd fucked a million women just like this. My wife looked like she'd never felt anything like this, and would do anything for more of it.

Her tight abs contracted. I loved watching that. She sat up a little. Her legs were still spread. She was still fucking BBD's dick just as much as he was fucking her pussy. But she was sitting up, bringing her face closer to his. His sweat was dripping down from his face onto her pert little Asian breasts.

She said something to him in Korean. She covered her mouth, like she was shy. He laughed and said something back and nodded.

What were they talking about? Were they making a secret plan?

She sat up more. She opened her mouth. He pushed his mouth at hers. She closed her eyes and sucked on his upper lip, then his lower lip.

They were kissing? She was actually kissing him? She barely even kissed me, her husband.

She was gyrating his pussy on his dick as she kissed him. He glanced at me. He definitely glanced at me. Then he stuck his tongue into her mouth.

They french-kissed, making out as they fucked. Her hands ran all over his back, and his hands fondled her tight ass cheeks.

I couldn't believe it. A little fun on the weekends, ok, fine — but Yoona was making out with this stud like he was her lover. She never kissed me like that. What was worse, I could never kiss her as passionately and skillfully as this man was kissing her.

I wasn't only useless at fucking. I wasn't only too poor to buy a bottle. I didn't even know how to kiss my wife.

Slowly, he pulled his lips away from my wife's face. He stuck his tongue out. Yoona glanced at me as the tip of her tongue met the tip of BBD's tongue. They played with their tongues in the air, laughing, as the crowd cheered.

BBD pulled away a bit and nodded to me. He actually pointed at me. "That's how you kiss a woman." Then he laughed again, showing all his white teeth. "Well, no, that's not how *you* kiss a woman. That's how *I* kiss a woman."

He looked away. He didn't even care to see my reaction.

He kissed her again. She threw her head back in pleasure. His blood-red lips roamed her delicate Asian face. He kissed her cheeks, her chin, her forehead, her neck, as she moaned in pleasure. He put his nose on her and inhaled her. And he was still jackhammer-fucking her pussy.

She looked into his eyes and said something in Korean. I didn't know what it was. Again. He kissed her again, this time passionately. Their lips were locked. Their eyes were wide open. My wife was staring deeply into this man's eyes. She'd never looked at me like that.

She slid her feet to wrap her legs completely around his torso. He was fucking her faster and faster.

He put his hands under her head and held her head up as he kissed her and ran his hands through his hair.

She shrieked. Her body bucked. She shook all over. She was fucking his dick even faster, more frantically, than he was fucking her. Her body was completely flushed red. Her nipples looked like tall pink mushrooms. She was cumming hard.

She grabbed his balls and fondled and pulled on them like she was milking all the fertile black cum out of them. His glutes shook and pumped in staccato. He roared and growled in orgasm. It was loud enough to hear even as lips were locked on my wife's lips and his tongue roamed my wife's mouth.

His whole body shook as he jackhammered his dick deep into my wife's pussy. His balls pumped. His whole lower body was pumping his cum into my wife. Even when his dick was still in her, she was overfilled with his cum. His hot salty cum was dripping out of her tight Asian pussy.

He growled again and grabbed her legs and spread them apart. He pushed one last time deep into her and pumped his last rope of cum into her. He exhaled deeply and brought his hands down under the small of Yoona's back. He held her closer as he lay his huge muscular body on top of my wife.

Yoona grabbed his dick to hold it inside her. "Don't take it out. Stay here with me." She looked into his eyes again and kissed him. He kissed her, turning his face to the side as they made out like lovers. Or made out like the lovers they were.

BBD whispered something in her ear. Yoona looked over at me, covered her mouth, and laughed. She wrapped her arms around BBD's huge black torso, embraced him lovingly, and stared deep into his eyes. She sighed, then passionately kissed him again.

I left.

Five

Two years married. Three years dating before that.

That was all I was allowed of Yoona, apparently. Now she was no longer mine.

On that drizzly Los Angeles night, I stood outside Slam, staring down into my phone. I didn't even mind my shirt was getting wet. I had bigger things to worry about. Worse things had happened that evening. I had to think hard to think about anything other than a stranger fucking Yoona, a stranger making love to her, a stranger kissing her — and her enjoying it more than she'd ever enjoyed being with me.

Would I even endure the humiliation of a divorce? Would she even return my calls? Was I so insignificant to her that she'd totally forget me, not even give me the dignity of a divorce.

I still loved her. But whether she was still mine wasn't my decision to make. A black stud, clearly my superior, had just taken her away from me. Right from under my nose. As I stood watching.

I forced myself to tap on the Uber icon. I forced myself to order the car. Five minutes away. I had five minutes to stand there, alone, in front of the club where my wife had left me.

How many passengers? Just one. I was going home alone.

Footsteps came rushing out of the club. A hand on my shoulder. "Sir! Your wallet!" It was the waiter. I'd dropped my wallet on the floor somehow. He handed it back to me. He was smirking a little.

I thanked him. I couldn't afford to tip him. The grin on his face only expanded.

Of course he knew what was up. How could he not have known? I deserved the humiliation. Even if I was a research chemist about to get his PhD, this waiter was that far above me, in everything. Not to mention how far above me was the big black man who'd just taken my wife away from me as I watched.

My phone beeped. A text from my Uber driver: *5 mins more. Sorry, rain.*

I messaged back: *Ok.* It was how my life went. Ok to everything. I had no room to turn it down. What could I have done — told him I would walk home? What could I have done inside that club — somehow tried to be more virile, richer, more masculine, more worthy of my wife's affections than that big black superman was?

Yeah fucking right. I had enough trouble paying the minimum payment on my credit card bill.

I hid my hands in my pockets.

Some clubbers who were leaving the place turned around and looked at me as they walked past. I must've been kind of famous: the hapless cuckold who'd just watched a big hairy black man fuck his hot little Asian wife. The hapless cuckold who was powerless to do anything about it. The hapless cuckold who had arrived at the club with his wife and now was going home alone.

Footsteps ran up to me again. What else could I have possibly left in the club?

"Why did you leave like that?" Yoona wrapped her arms around me. She kissed my lips before I could even answer.

"You — aren't you—" I looked back at the club entrance. "Where's BBD?"

"That creep wouldn't leave me alone." She sighed and shook her head. "He was trying to get me to go home with him."

"And you didn't go with him?" I looked at her. She was staring into my eyes.

"Why would I do that?" She shook her head. That black hair was again airborne. It was gorgeous, even in the dim light of an LA street corner at midnight. "You're my man. You know that."

The Uber pulled up. I opened the door for her. She slid inside. I followed.

"For Danny?" The driver looked up in the rear view mirror.

"Yup." I nodded.

"For Danny and his gorgeous Asian supermodel companion?" The driver smiled and nodded. He was appreciating Yoona. Like any heterosexual man would.

"I guess." I had no reason to continue the conversation.

She pulled me closer to her side of the seat, then grabbed my shoulders and drew my face close to hers. "Danny. You're my man. You're always my man."

She kissed me. Hard. Even harder than she'd kissed BBD up on stage.

I was drunk on the feeling of her tongue exploring my mouth, her lips on mine, all my wife's pheromones and womanly smells washing over me. I thought I'd never experience that again. I kissed her as passionately as she kissed me. Yoona stared into my eyes. The driver pulled away from the club.

Suddenly, I drew my mouth away. It didn't feel right. Why had she turned down BBD?

I looked away from her eyes. It would've been too confrontational to look at her directly. "I don't understand why you didn't go home with him."

"You're my husband, Danny." She licked inside my ear. I laughed with the tickling feeling of it. My dick rose to diamond-hard erection. "I only love you."

"But I don't have—"

"What don't you have, Danny?" Her mouth was at my crotch. She was so quick and familiar with the way she unzipped my pants. She knew exactly where to go. Her shiny red fingernails were inside my pants in seconds. My dick was out of my pants. Her red lips were on it before I even really processed what was going on.

"Oh, fuck." I leaned far back in the seat. Her tongue was running up and down my shaft. She swirled her tongue around my dickhead while she stared up into my eyes in the dark of the Uber car's back seat.

"I love sucking your dick, Danny." She smiled up at me. She cupped my balls as she slid my dick back into her mouth. She bobbed her head up and down on it. Her slurps were loud. The driver looked like he was concerned, disgusted, and interested, all at once.

"After watching you in the club—" I tried to control my breathing and relax all the muscles in my body. "I'm too close to cumming. I was so turned on from watching you get fucked by BBD.'

Yoona gently let my dick out of her mouth. Still cradling it in her fingers, she lifted her face to mine. "I was thinking of you the whole time, Danny. I love you."

She kissed me. Again. Her tongue dove furiously into my mouth and ran over my teeth. She'd never kissed me like that before.

I grabbed at her silky smooth thigh under her dress. Under her panties, I cupped her ass in my palm.

"Danny, I'm so fucking horny for you." She frantically kissed my nose, my chin, my ears, and my lips as she peeled off her dress, then her bra, then her panties.

I palmed at the cool, soft skin of her thighs, her ass, her midsection, her breasts. I wanted to take every part of her.

Yoona was totally naked in the back seat of this Uber car speeding down the I-5. She grabbed my unzipped pants and pulled them down until they were at my knees.

"You ready?" There was her mischievous grin again.

"You mean—"

"Feel my cunt." She grabbed my hand and patted it on her sopping wet pussy. Or cunt.

"That's wet." I inhaled deeply.

She whispered in my ear: "So let's go. Fuck me, Danny. Fuck me better and harder than any other man ever could."

In that moment, I was sure I was capable of it. Even if my dick wasn't the biggest, it felt like the biggest. Even if I wasn't the strongest, with Yoona's eyes of desire fixed on me, I felt like I was the strongest man who'd ever walked the earth.

Yoona brought one long leg over me, and the other on the other side of me. She was straddling me, kneeling on the edge of the car seat.

She moved her face in to mine and kissed my lips. At the same time, she brought her pussy down onto my hard dick.

I fucked her. I fucked her hard. I ran my hands up and down her naked back and kissed every inch of her face and neck and I thrust my dick up as deep as I could into her. She moaned with every one of my deep thrusts up into her.

I brought my hand down to where our pubes met and fingered her clit, rubbing it back and forth. She moaned in pleasure and recoiled with her whole body, drawing my cock farther into her pussy.

My hands under her perfectly tight, smooth Asian ass cheeks, I raised her up and lowered her again on my dick. Faster and faster. I was pouring sweat and so was she.

The driver stared straight ahead as she drove. While I was kissing Yoona, I caught him glancing at us through the mirror. He must've loved seeing my wife's gorgeous naked body: what he never could have.

"Fuck me, Danny," Yoona whispered in my ear. She nibbled at my earlobe and grabbed at my nipples with her lithe fingers.

I felt the orgasm welling up deep inside me. My balls felt like they were about to explode.

Yoona closed her eyes and bit down on her lip. She shook all over as she rode my dick. Her pussy was so hot; it was like keeping my dick in an oven.

"I'm cumming!" She squealed and grabbed down to reach at my balls. When she tugged on my balls, I felt like a real man.

My thighs spasmed and shook. I shot cum up into her. I shot rope after rope. She was smiling and kissing me.

I thrust up again, deeper into her, and shot another rope. Then another one. My cum was spilling out of her pussy. She wrapped her arms around me and drew herself closer and closer to me, her small firm breasts pressing up against my shoulder blades as she rode my dick.

I spurted the last few ropes of cum into her. It spilled out of her pussy onto my crotch. I'd have to pay an Uber cleaning fee. I didn't care.

Yoona took her phone out of her bag. She put it on selfie mode. Before I could even say anything, she'd taken a picture of the two of us, entwined in an embrace, in post-orgasmic bliss.

Yoona's mischievous grin came over her face again. "I'm gonna WhatsApp this to BBD." She clicked and tapped on the phone as she grinded her pussy on my softening dick. My cum was spilling out of her pussy, all over my crotch and balls.

"Why?" I shrugged and kissed her again.

"To tell him how much better you are than him." She bit my shoulder, then kissed my lips again and pushed her pussy farther onto my softening dick. She slowly licked across my lips while staring into my eyes. "And how much I love you. And how you're the best husband I could ever imagine."

"Really?" It almost sounded too good to be true. Almost.

"Really. I love you so much and you're so much better than that big brute ever could be." Yoona kissed me again. She clicked on the Send button on her phone. Then she waved the phone at me. "But I have his number."

Afterword

Join the Travis Mayfair VIP Club:

Asian hotwife fun, delivered very discreetly to your email.

No spam, no explicit emails, I don't share your address, and you can unsubscribe anytime.

http://eepurl.com/gRZ04T

Printed in Great Britain
by Amazon

64664660R00038